15 Short Stories

GRANDMA'S LEGACY

And Other Stories

Ogork Kate Taku

i

GRANDMA'S LEGACY

First edition 2016

© Ogork Catherine, 2016

Tel: 699813186

E-mail: kateogork@yahoo.com

ISBN: 978-9956-744-58-1

Typeset and formatted by A and A Virtual Computer Shop, Buea.

Tel: (237) 676 281 106 /(237) 676 442 005

Email: aavirtualcs@gmail.com

Printed, Bound and Published in Cameroon by
SHILOH PRINTERS, Buea
Tel: (237) 677 755 809

THOUGHT OF THE YEAR

The best portion of a good man's life: His little,
Nameless unremembered acts of kindness and love.

(William Wordsworth)

DEDICATION

To my beloved husband, Dr. Besong Ntui OGORK.

For all these years you've been an extraordinary

pillar on whom I lean for support and inspiration.

You have stimulated my brainwave timelessly

And awakened the flame of knowledge in me.

I will forever appreciate your endless

love and support.

Thank you.

ACKNOWLEDGEMENT

This work would not have come to its fruitfulness if some special persons had not taken off time to contribute in one way or another to its realization.

I am therefore incalculably thankful to God Almighty for giving me the good health and guidance throughout these years.

Special thanks go to my special friend and colleague, Mr. Arrey-Njok Tabe Takang who painstakingly criticized the work and pictures, did the assembling of the stories and also made useful directions on publishing.

I equally want to appreciate my spiritual leader, the Rev. Ebai Gustav for accepting to write the foreword to this collection during a time when he was aggrieved with the loss of his sister. His electrifying sermons equally formed the base for these motivational stories.

I am very grateful to my daughter, Ogork M'Agbornaw, for taking time off to read through the manuscript. Her observations really shaped the final product of these stories, and I remain appreciative of her continuous encouragement through her own studies.

And to where charity begins, I am forever thankful to my immediate family. First to my husband who bore my absences and late nights up without whining; and then to my kids, Ebob, M'Agbornaw, Atungu and Besong-aya for their encouragement that pushed me to publish these stories .

PREFACE

In my youthful days, a story-telling session was one of the best moments during the holiday. It often took place in the evenings when everyone had finished their house chores and individual tasks. Our mother, of course, was the incubator of the tales, both fiction and non-fiction. It did not bother us how many times she told the same story because even though the stories were familiar, their songs were always enjoyable and involving. Each folktale had a moral value that it taught and each riddle was always a puzzle. The myths and legends were the best stories for we were always marveled by the bravery and heroism of the gods/ goddesses. All these legendary stories contributed in shaping our minds about the past and its history and instilled some cultural values and thoughts in me.

Those days are far gone now and most of those traditional values are lost. Modernism and globalisation have taken over the fireside stories and the mother-tongue has become endangered. It is high time therefore, that Africans come up with other strategies to implant some moral values in the young and feeble minds of their children. If traditional oral tales cannot be told, then modern tales that teach aspects of African morality have to be used.

It is with these thoughts that I decided to make a collection of stories that end with some moral values, stories that will ignite the reading culture in the youths and imbibe some norms into their psyche. It is my ultimate wish that the reception of these stories will meet my expectations.

Ogork Kate

FOREWORD

Story telling is a huge part of human culture. Whatever we know about ourselves, whatever has been passed down and whatever we pass on or will pass down; it is certain that the greatest part of it is and will always be through story telling.

It is difficult to draw a line between Education and story-telling because from Early Man, through the various religious and scientific creation stories; and the inventions through human conquests and settlement and looking at all stages of human life and legacy, we find only one common source of education – story telling.

Teaching through stories is innate or inborn. Nobody taught the other about it. Every culture just seemed to practice it naturally. I guess, it is expected especially as God Himself is the greatest story teller.

Today, technology has made story telling more important and alive than ever. The Western world strives daily to inspire by their heroic tales, portraying selfless heroes and defenders of peace and justice. Stories are told through books, theatre, and motion pictures (movies) as ways that inspire creativity, a drive towards greatness. Children are made to believe that anyone can be a superhero. In Africa, however the great stories that used to inspire good conduct, righteousness and working for the common good have been replaced with the glorification of bad behaviour, ritualistic and occultist practices; teaching youths about taking the easy way out.

That is why a book like **GRANDMA'S LEGACY** *And Other Stories* is a necessity to our present age. In this age of psycho-emotional experts where anyone writes and says what they want through the Internet, where our children and youths access them and take these stories as gospel, we need stories that will inspire us and bring back lost morals.

Kate Ogork has written simple, yet very profound stories that transcend religion, age and tradition. Stories that can truly inspire and challenge our morality. She has also added the moral lesson behind each story, which should help everyone understand many situations in life.

GRANDMA'S LEGACY *And Other Stories,* is a book for family reading. It can also be used as bedtime stories for the kids.

I can imagine how the characters of our children can be molded positively if they go to bed thinking or having in mind such great moral lessons.

I remember the primary school song "Storytelling is part of our culture…… The Bible is a testimony that even God uses storytelling as the main form of education. Read the stories in this book diligently and joyfully and you will be enriched abundantly.

May God speak to you who read this book, through the inspirational stories herein.

Thank you KATE OGORK, for this book, *GRANDMA'S LEGACY And Other Stories*

Rev. EBAI Gustav TABI
Secretaire Executif DIC
CEPCA _ Yaounde

CONTENTS

1   GRANDMA'S LEGACY

You may never know how your life will end here on earth and who will be by your side on the last day. Many people are afflicted, with friends and relatives to take care of them; others remain healthy, with or without friends or children. Life is very unpredictable.

There lived a very beautiful lady in one of the small towns in the Southern Region of Cameroon. Her name was Henrietta. Henrietta got married quite young; in fact, she got married as a kid – fifteen years old. God blessed her with eight children, six girls and two boys. She was very industrious, and without depending on her husband, she raised her children to become teachers, carpenters, hairdressers and business-men. God's light later shone on her children and they started going abroad one after the other, some to England, others to Germany and yet others to Belgium. There was total joy in her home.

Before long invitations started pouring in. Henrietta's children wanted her to visit and live with them abroad. She flew to all ends of the world. Her name changed from 'Mami Koki' to 'Bush Faller'. Everyone admired her and wished to be in her shoes. Henrietta sometimes spent seven months in, and five months out of the country. Life was sweet.

'Bush Faller' soon realized that she preferred her home to being abroad. She told her kids that she had grandchildren to take care of; and her husband and friends to look after. Her first child had left behind two kids before travelling abroad, her second child left one and they needed her attention; but of all her concerns, she had to take care of her adopted grand daughter who lived with her. To tell you the truth, she knew neither this child's father nor mother. Someone had brought the baby to her and she had named her Naomi. This was when Naomi was just six months old. Henrietta was sitting in front of her house one morning. A young girl came to her and asked if she could help with the baby while she went behind to relief herself. Henrietta took the baby and the girl passed by her and went to the back of the compound.

The girl never returned. Henrietta waited until evening but there was no sign of the young girl. She took the baby to the police who left her under Henrietta's custody. Since then, she did not know where to turn to and ask questions about the child. She had raised Naomi for twelve years to a respectful, hardworking and cheerful girl; always happy and always smiling. They were so fond of each other.

Naomi knew everything about Grandma – the drugs Grandma took and at what time, all her meeting attires, her friends' houses, her favourite meals, everything. Naomi's most cherished moment was when she sat next to her Grandma, singing or listening to adult conversations.

On this faithful day Naomi and Grandma were in the kitchen preparing lunch. They had just finished pounding cocoyam and Grandma was busy with the soup. She was sitting on a low stool inside the wood kitchen to ease her work, while Naomi sat on a stone outside telling Grandma about a story that she read.

Naomi was demonstrating what a boy in the story did when she heard a scream and a loud rattling. She turned just on time to see her Grandma slumbering to the kitchen floor. Naomi jumped and caught her, trying to hold her upright, but Grandma's weight was too much for little Naomi. She placed Grandma gently on the kitchen floor, rushed outside and shouted for help.

Neighbours immediately rushed to the scene and tried administering the little first aid they could remember, but they quickly realized that the case was too serious for them to handle. Grandma could talk no more, she could not respond to noises around her. In fact, she could not even open her eyes. What had happened so suddenly!!!

Naomi gently placed Grandma on the Kitchen floor.

Grandma was rushed to the hospital with a multitude of friends and relatives scuttling to the scene to find out what was happening, but barely thirty minutes later, she was declared dead. Grandma had died of heart attack!

The whole compound was filled with mourners. People somersaulted like athletes in a competition. No one could believe the news; many said they saw her at morning mass at 5:00am; some said they had met in the market and even chatted that same morning, and yet others said she gave them breakfast of left-over food. How then could someone die without being sick?

Meanwhile, Naomi had been moving round the compound wailing. On each hand she was still holding Grandma's slippers which she had picked and taken to the hospital. No one had noticed her, but attention was drawn towards her when close to an hour after everyone had stopped, Naomi was still crying. People tried to stop her, but she would not stop weeping.

"What do I do now ehhhh?

Who will be my Grandmother again?

Where do I go from here?

Someone help me oooh! I am finished!!!

My Grandmother is not dead oooh, don't leave her at the mortuary, bring her back home oooh, bring Grandma home!!!"

She went on and on. "My Grandma is my friend, Grandma is my mother, she is my father ooohhh, I have no one else. Who will send me to school? Who will buy my books? Who will sing and I dance eehhh? I am finished!!!"

For two days Naomi wept nonstop, taking short breaks when people scolded and threatened to send her to Grandma's friend. By evening on the second day Naomi came down with a very high fever. She was shivering from head to toe; and was put in bed and given medication, but each time she became conscious of her surroundings again, she started crying.

I tell you, when Mami Koki died, none of her eight children were present to mourn her. They loved their mother and had taken good care of her, yet were hundreds of kilometers away; only Naomi was there at her side. She was left behind to tell Grandma's story first hand as she had lived it until death snatched her away. Grandma had written a book in Naomi's life and left for everyone to see or read.

What legacy are you leaving behind dear reader? Who will weep for you when you exit this world? Do you show love only to your biological children? They may not be there for you when you need them most. They may not even have stories to tell about you because they take your love for granted.

Do not hesitate, my friend, show love to someone today! Do the little good you can, it will not change you or your finances, but the good you show today will live with you and live after you. Leave behind a legacy. Let people mourn your absence, not rejoice on your demise. Show love to people, especially to the deprived, and God will bless you lavishly.

QUESTIONS

1. a) How old is Naomi?

   b) What makes you know her age?

2. Name some leisure activities that Naomi enjoyed with Grandma.

3. Chose two words from the story that have the same number of syllables as the word 'biological'.

4. What lesson(s) have you learnt from this story?

2   PAUL'S CROSS

Njom Paul was an energetic, fun-filled and spirited young man . He lived in Mafola, a small city near the capital of his country. Paul was an accountant and had graduated from Kingston Memorial College, a very prestigious University in his country. He got a job with a small company and decided that he would settle with that for a short while before looking for a better job, after all, everyone has to start from some-where.

After working for two years, Paul decided to get married. He was very lucky and fell on a beauti-ful, well-behaved and hardworking girl whose name was Pauline. She too was a graduate with a degree in Law, but did not have a job yet. The pair was a wonderful one, admired by their friends and well-loved by both families. They went to church together, attended meetings together, walked around town together and often attended to invitations together.

After two years of marriage, Paul and Pauline were blessed with a son. He was named after Paul's father, Joseph. Then three years later, another baby was born into the family, this time a beautiful girl who took so much after her dad. He decided to name her Paulette. And so Joseph and Paulette became the centre of attention in that home. Everyone who met the couple would ask after the children and implore them to raise the kids in the African style with no excesses. The couple did their best and their kids were very healthy and always cheerful.

When Paulette turned four, however, her parents noticed that she was getting sick quite often in spite of the continuous care and attention given her. She was in the kindergarten and had to get up earlier than she often did so as to prepare for school. They decided to let her sleep and go to school late, but Paulette was still sick every other week. She grew very pale and weak, and became less active; she was always anemic and had to be placed on blood tonic. Even her brother was not happy because he did not have someone to run around with any more. It was so frustrating for Joseph to see Paulette lying on the couch in the living room or admitted in the hospital, or worse still, being forced to take her medications. He did not like it at all.

After a few months, little Paulette was diagnosed with the Sickle Cell disease. Her parents were told that it was a red blood cell disorder and was a condition that she had to live with all through her life. They just had to be more observant of her meals and make sure she did not go through a lot of stress.

This was heart-breaking for the young couple. They cried each time their daughter was suffering from pains in her joints. They stayed up with her at night, taking turns to calm and massage her. Pauline could not take her part-time teaching job seriously anymore because she was in the hospital with her daughter too often. Paul was not steady at his work place and was given verbal warnings several times, all because of his daughter's condition. It was becoming too hard for them to bear.

By the age of twelve it was very clear that Paulette was physically smaller than other children of her age. She was very thin and frail; she could not do much work at home and had an artificial fair complexion that looked transparent. Whenever other kids were playing she just sat around watching them, and talking very sparingly. Paulette was often feeble and skipped school very often. Her friends, class-mates and teachers made it a duty to visit her regularly either at home or in the hospital when they did not see her in school for long. But Paulette was a very good baby-sitter to her kid sister who was then just three years old. Paulette was not only a caring sister, she was also intelligent, focused and very smart. Her teachers knew that she was not very regular at school because of ill-health, but she spent time studying at home and was always among the first top five in her class.

A few years later, Paul became so frustrated with his daughter's continuous ill-health. He blamed his wife for every little thing that went wrong in the house; told her how she was a good-for-nothing wife who bore him only kids that drained all his money. He became nagging and very rude, especially to his wife's family members. He did not want to pay Paulette's hospital bills anymore, saying she was better off dead than alive; and then he started keeping late nights.

Then one day Paul went to the Lord in prayer. He was on his kneels for so long, whispering inaudible words and tears running down his cheeks that his wife had to intervene for him to get up. In his prayer he complained to God that his life was too difficult for him to continue. He told God that his job was not good enough, his wife did not work, and his daughter was too sick to be considered a child. He told God that he could no longer bear the cross of his daughter; that the cross was too heavy for him and God should take it away. If God didn't want to take it completely, he should give him a lighter cross.

That night Paul had a dream. In the dream he was with his colleague and they went out to visit some sick persons. First they went to a psychiatric home. Paul saw so many people suffering from mental problems, among them children. He was particularly interested in one boy who was about fifteen, very tall and calm, but very aggressive. They were told that there were about twelve juveniles in that center who were suffering from the same problem. His friend turned to him and asked Paul how he'll feel if that were his son. Paul turned and quickly ran out of the room. He did not want to consider such thoughts.

Then they went to the hospital. At the children's ward they met so many kids, some attended to by their mothers, others by their fathers and some by their siblings. Paul's eyes fell on a little girl who was about six years old. She was looking very cheerful, but could neither get out of bed nor could she talk. She was suffering from Autism. Her mother told them that she was her only child, and she gave thanks to God everyday for giving her that child because there were some who didn't even have. Paul's countenance changed. "How could someone be happy with such a sick child, when he could not cope with his daughter?" he wondered to himself,

Next they visited the surgical unit. There were so many patients that Paul wanted to just run out and go back home, but his friend would not let him. They saw some kids who had undergone operations and were battling between life and death. Their parents were weeping and comforting each other. In another ward were those whose body parts had been amputated - some hands, others legs. They would have to live without these parts for the rest of their lives.

At the far end of that ward, Paul saw a little girl who looked exactly like his daughter Paulette. She was smiling graciously and cuddling her younger sister. Paul ran to her and held out his hand to pick up the girl whom he considered was his daughter, but a voice shouted behind him, "don't touch her, she's my daughter." Paul was shocked.

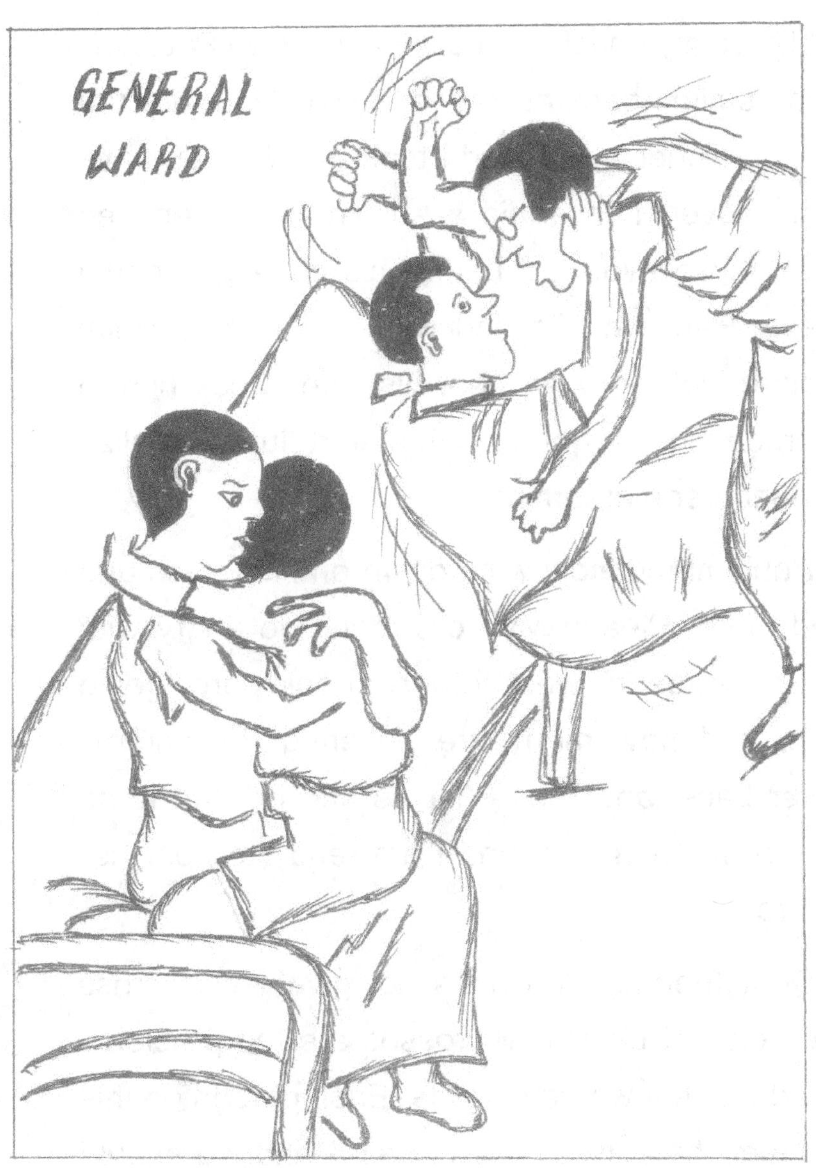

Paul was fighting with the man to claim back his daughter.

"That's my daughter," he said, "my own Paulette". The man smiled back at Paul and said "you rejected her and gave her away, and I took her. So you have no claim over her again." An argument ensued between these two, and before his colleague could intervene, Paul was fighting with the man to claim back his daughter. Just then, his wife shook him to stop screaming. He got up with a start, just to realize that he had been dreaming.

Paul immediately went down on his knees and begged God. "Please My Lord, don't be angry with me. I have seen what other people are going through, and how many are suffering. I want my daughter back, and I love her as she is. She is no burden to me anymore, and I am ready to bear her as my cross."

Dear friends, God does not give you a cross that you cannot bear. Our crosses are the problems and burdens that we have in life. Each person on this planet earth has his/her own burden and we should never compare our tribulations to those of others.

When you have a problem, pray and God will take care of it, for God gives each man according to his means and ability.

Paulette grew up to become the pride of her family. Stronger and less sickling. As a Pediatrician, she is now helping to care for other kids.

QUESTIONS

1. What are the professions of Paul and Pauline?

2. How many characters are in this story?

3. Give three (3) things that Paul and his wife do in common as a couple that made people admire them.

4. Spell out the following words used in the passage correctly:
    a) Duragate
    b) Sdneirf
    c) Laup
    d) Terdaugh

5. What is the cross that Paul had to bear?

6. Describe what you would do as a student in order to succeed like Paulette.

7. Go back to the picture and:
    a) Name all the characters.
    b) Colour their outfits so as to differentiate each character.

3   THE HOMELESS MAN

Sometimes God sends situations our way to remind us of how blessed we are! Other times God may just be opening our eyes to the many problems that people face on earth. When we therefore meet someone, we should think twice before judging the person.

My name is Therese and I am going to recount a real life experience that I faced some months ago. One evening as I was leaving Mahima, a shop in the center of the city, I noticed a man going through the garbage can outside the stop. As I walked to my car I watched him as he reached into the garbage can and pulled out trash bags and inspected all that was in the thrown away bags. He did this for several minutes. He would find a few left-overs in one bag and a bite or two of some bread or 'bobolo' in another bag. I had seen him twice or thrice before, but on this day I was particularly concerned, I can not say why.

The man never bothered anyone, and did not stop and beg for money as people entered and left the shop. He was scavenging the trash cans but I noticed he did not look mad. After he went through the entire trash, he neatly cleaned up the area and wrapped up the food he found in a dirty plastic paper, went to a little corner and sat down to eat whatever he had gathered out of the trash. My heart literally hurt for him. I am not someone who just hands out money or even helps homeless people, you know, because so many are not truly homeless. In fact, there is a belief in my culture that beggars are Satan's agents sent on earth to bring hardship to those who pity and help them. So, many people just ignore them; and I have always done so until this fateful day.

I knew that I had to help him. I got out of my car, walked to the man and asked him if I could buy him something to eat. He told me that he would appreciate anything I could get for him. So I asked him to follow me so I could buy him a meal at the fast food kiosk around the bakery. He followed me and I bought him the biggest meal they had on the menu. The only request he gave for his order was for me to get him a big bottle of soft drink to go with his meal!

When I handed him his food, he was so thankful. He told me his name was Robert and that he had been homeless ever since his sister died about a year ago. His sister, he said, was the only one left in his family who was of help to him. She bought his drugs, paid his rents and made sure she fed him at least once a day; but death came from nowhere and snatched her away. She was not sick at all, she just collapsed one afternoon in the office and died even before the doctor could attend to her.

Robert mourned that it would have been better for him who had been sick for so long to die. "I have no one else to rely on and no one to feed me," he lamented. He was trying to get off the garbage can, but it was so hard. He told me again how much he appreciated the meal.

I noticed he did not look mad.

When I got back into my car, I drove off with such heaviness in my heart for this man. I drove down the road and felt compelled to go back and help him. When I went back he had finished his meal and was walking away. I pulled up beside him and asked him if there was any way I could help him. He told me not really. He asked neither for money nor my name. So I asked him if I could buy him a few meals and leave for him. He told me that would be so kind. I therefore looked for an eating house some-where nearby, paid for some meals and told the owner to feed him each day until the money ran out.

Robert broke down crying. He said he had prayed for me today! I was not sure what he meant (I was assuming he was praying for me for what I did for him) so I thanked him. But he said, "No, you don't understand. I prayed that God would send someone to buy me a hot meal today… and he sent you!" I didn't know what to say… I was speechless! Praying for a hot meal wasn't a prayer I had prayed today! Come to think of it, that is not a prayer I have ever prayed before! I always pray over my food, but I've never prayed for a meal… it's expected! I've never doubted that I would not be able to eat… Tears began to fill my eyes! Oh my… how blessed am I… Maybe God used me to answer this man's prayer, and to let him know that He cares for him and knows what he's going through! Or, maybe God used this man to show me just how blessed I am and to know the things I take for granted.

He said, "You see, I have umbilical hernia!" He pulled up his shirt and pointed to a huge mass that was poking out from his stomach. He said he knew it would not be much longer, especially since he did not take medications any more. I asked him if he knew Jesus and he said that he did. I asked if I could pray with him and he said that I could. We prayed right there on the sidewalk of the road. Tears just poured from his eyes. Robert told me he knew that he was going to die and that he was ready to die. He was tired of being in pain and he would be better off dead because that was no life – living the way he did. I stayed and encouraged him for a few minutes, trying to fight back my own tears.

My joy is that the Holy Spirit helped me and I showed Robert the love of Jesus today; that something I said gave him hope. You see, everybody has a story! I know Robert's story now all because I felt compelled to help him, and he ended up touching me today!

When I left Robert, I knew that I had done what God wanted me to do! God put him in my path today… I know He did! I've never felt such a feeling to help someone as I did today. I was reminded again of how blessed I was! I have a vehicle that gets me from place to place, I have a roof over my head, clean clothes, money to buy my meals, running water, electricity, my health, a job, family, and friends! Others don't. Think about yourself too, and all the good things you have which others do not.

If you've read this far, please remember Robert and many others who are suffering from life-threatening diseases in your prayers! Remember the homeless and those living in misery.

QUESTIONS

1.   Complete the table below:

No	Adjective	Comparative	Superlative
a	Short		
b	Clean		
c	Many		
d	Good		
e	Expensive		
f	Much		
g	Far		

2.   Where is this story set?

3.   How many characters are in the story?

4.   What does the writer mean by "my heart literally hurt for him?

5.   Write down four(4) ways through which you can show love to the sick and needy.

4 VISIT TO THE ORPHANAGE

Helmine was a pretty little girl, a lone child to her parents. She got away with whatever she did wrong. She was always given whatever she demanded for. She had a room to herself, a car that took her to and from school, and a maid who attended to her every need. At 14, Helmine had never washed any of her own dresses, did not know how to cook or even fry an omelette, because her dad would not let her touch any sharp object for fear of her getting hurt.

All these made Helmine very arrogant and lazy. She would not accept even to remove her plate from the dining table, demanding that the steward does it and does the clean-up too.

Her mom thought her attitude was getting off hand and started scolding her daughter, forcing her to be in the kitchen with others and assigning her to do house chores. But Helmine would always look for an opportunity to dodge and allow others to do her chores.

At the age of fifteen Helmine was preparing to enter High School. She had all sorts of plans and laid them down to her father. She demanded a particular type of shoes, asked for her weekly allowance to be increased, her uniform to be sewn to a special style, and above all, she wanted to attend only a school that accepted girls to braid their hair. Her wishes, of course, were granted.

Then one fine Saturday in August Helmine's mother decided to pay a routine visit to an orphanage in the outskirts of the city. She bought some food items, school supplies and laundry stuff and put into her car, ready for the visit. As she was leaving the room Helmine asked if she could accompany her to the orphanage. Her mother asked her why she wanted to go and Helmine said because she was bored staying at home; to which her request was granted.

At the orphanage the children all gathered to receive their guests. There were over fifty-three of them ranging from two weeks old to nineteen years.

Most of them were shabbily dressed with either torn or completely worn out clothes. Some were playing around happily while others were sitting about looking malnourished and sad. The older girls were taking care of the babies, while the toddlers were left on their own. Helmine was dumb-founded.

Shortly after their arrival it was lunch time at the orphanage. Food was brought in for the younger kids and those from five years and above rushed to the kitchen to take theirs. When they settled down to eat, their "mother" led them in prayers and everyone started eating. Helmine noticed that the rice the children ate had just been simply boiled and some bleached palm oil mixed in it. There was no fish or meat, no tomato or veggies, and yet the children ate with so much appetite.

Before long a fight broke out between two girls of about eight and ten because one was picking grains of rice that had fallen on the floor in front of the other girl. She said it was hers and the other girl did not have to pick from 'her' space.

Helmine was watching with disbelief.

Helmine had been watching with disbelief. She could never have imagined that there were children her age who were in so much need. She thought of all the food and clothes she had back at home; all the demands she made which were granted; all the love lavished on her, yet there were many who were looking for someone to help give them just their basic needs. Tears rolled down her cheeks and she did not bother to wipe them off. Then she ran to the car and wept for about ten minutes. She did not return to the girls' camp for fear of breaking down again.

That evening when she got home, Helmine worked so hard in the kitchen that even her father was wondering what could have come over her. This lone visit changed Helmine completely and equally showed her the other side of life.

When you are blessed, do not look down on others; and remember to thank God for any situation that you find yourself in.

QUESTIONS

1. How many brothers and sisters does Helmine have? How do you know?

2. State three reasons why you think Helmine is a spoilt child.

3. Which of her parents would you say contributed more in making Helmine a spoilt child? Why do you think so?

4. What other lessons have you learnt from this story?

5. Go back to page 32 and colour the picture, making sure to use different colours to differentiate the characters.

5   YOU CAN MAKE IT

You may never know what causes some people to shine or excel in life. Some achieve greatness while others go to slumber. Sometimes people have neither the courage nor the will-power to do something, but the desire to help another person pushes them to unexpected results.

Martha was a 46-year-old woman who had been crippled for about five years following a road accident that took away the life of her two daughters. After spending seven months in the hospital, she had been discharged with numb limps on a wheel chair. Her husband had to stay away from work for one month so as to help her adjust to her new situation and learn to move about the house on the wheel chair.

Martha, however, refused to cooperate. She refused to accept her new condition and locked herself up from friends and relatives. She would not let anyone take her out of her position. Two years later, she still refused to go to church, rejected offers to visit friends or even to help with the upbringing of her two surviving kids. Her husband felt frustrated.

One evening in December, Martha's fourteen-year-old son, Bryan, was trying to prepare dinner for his seven-year-old brother when he heard a loud scream from the room. He abandoned the cooking and dashed into the bedroom that he shared with his brother, just on time to meet the latter on the bed face to face with a very huge snake. The snake had somehow been hanging on the roof unnoticed, and had then dropped on the bed. It crawled towards the little boy; and as he tried to run, his leg had hit the tail of the snake and the snake turned and bit him. That was when he screamed and his brother ran in.

Bryan could not withstand the sight of the snake. He shouted at the top of his voice,

"mommmm, a snake!!!" no response.
Bryan ran to the corner of the room, grapped

whatever he could find and went for the snake in full attack. The battle was a hard one for him alone; and with his brother on the bed, he was careful not to hurt him.

"Jump out of the bed!!!" he instructed his brother. But the kid was too weak from pain to move. He simply said, "help me, Bryan, help me!" and then collapsed on the bed.

By this time the snake had slipped into the sheets and out of sight. Bryan was now torn between moving his brother and looking for the snake which was still a potential danger to both of them. Just then he shouted again, "Mommmmm, a snake!!! Mom, momm, Lesley is dying." He broke out in tears.

Martha jumped out of the wheelchair she was sitting on. She stumbled twice or thrice and fell. Crawled to the room door and shouted "I'm here, what is wrong with Lesley?"

Bryan had Lesley on his arms and was weeping, "wake up Lesley, wake up." Just then

Bryan noticed the snake moving again. He quickly deposited his brother on his mother's arms with the instruction "run, mommm, runnn!" Then he picked an umbrella that was in the room and started hitting the portion of the bed where he saw the movement. He hit tirelessly until the movement stopped.

By the time Bryan ran out to attend to Lesley, Martha was trying to board a taxi. She had somehow walked and somehow crawled to the road. They dashed into the taxi and headed for the hospital. When the doctor who was attending to the little boy came back and announced that Lesley was out of danger, Martha jumped from the corner and hugged Bryan, wiping off tears and thanking her son for being so brave and bold.

"What!!!" Bryan took a second look at his mom again. "God, this is your making!!! Mom, you can walk!!! You can walk!!!" Martha turned and looked down at her legs, realizing for the first time that she was on her feet!! Walking!!!

Martha was trying to board a taxi. She had somehow
walked and somehow crawled to the road.

Just then her husband rushed into the hospital's emergency room, panting from fright and exhaustion. He came to an abrupt stop when he saw his wife. "You on your feet? You can walk?". Martha's husband was shocked. The desire to safe her son had pushed Martha to her feet.

Get up my friend, from that problem that has been holding you hostage for so long. Get out of your comfort zone and face the challenges of life. Do not give up in life dear reader, for unless you struggle to overcome your difficulties, you will remain stagnant. Yes, Faith without action is dead. We can only have a transformed life if we believe in ourselves and take action.

QUESTIONS

1. What caused Martha to remain on the wheel chair?

2. What in your opinion forced Martha to leave her wheel chair?

3. Give another meaning for the following words:
   a. Numb
   b. Cooperate
   c. Crawled
   d. Hugged

4. In one paragraph say how Bryan succeeds in killing the snake.

5. "You can walk?" who asked this question and why?

6. What lessons do we learn from this story?

A CALL FOR HELP

Adeline was driving downtown to visit her sister one evening when it started drizzling. She stopped the car, went round to her three-year-old daughter who was sitting at the back seat and belted her firmly to the car seat. She then returned to the driver's seat and continued her trip.

A few kilometers away, the rain became more serious, and only grew heavier and heavier until she could barely see the road. She slowed down and was thinking of turning off her engine to wait for the rain to subside. Just then an oncoming car narrowly missed hitting her because the driver too could not see clearly. She then thought to herself that it was more dangerous waiting on one spot; so she continued, this time even slower.

Just a few meters away from the previous spot, Adeline realized that rain water had covered the entire road. She was virtually driving in a pool, her windscreen was clouded and she could not see a thing. She pulled to the side and waited, but then her daughter started crying. The kid was frightened by the heavy downpour and wanted some company. The raindrops hit so hard on the car that Adeline thought it would leave a dent.

Adeline tried to stop her daughter from crying to no avail. She could not go out to unbelt her because the rain was extremely heavy. In fact, she could not even hear herself when she spoke. When she realized that her daughter was getting too hysteric, Adeline decided to drive on for two reasons; first of all her sister's house was just about fifteen minutes away, and secondly, where she was stationed was unsafe because there were no houses around the vicinity. She drove off.

By this time it was dusk already. She turned on her lights because it was raining and she also wanted oncoming drivers to be able to see her. The rain had subsided and much of the water had dried up, but the road was very slippery. Each time she turned the vehicle, it slid off the road and then balanced again. She became scared.

Then at that moment, she saw an oncoming truck. How she would manage on that narrow road preoccupied her thoughts. The truck was on high speed and the driver did not care about other cars. It was coming straight ahead of her. Adeline swayed to one corner to avoid the truck, but she was too close to the sidewalk. Her car slipped off the road, somersaulted into the nearby valley and went out of sight. Everything was quiet.

The truck driver had driven off, unaware of the accident. No car was plying the road because of the bad weather; and so no one knew that there was a car in the ditch nearby.

Meanwhile, Adeline's sister waited for a very long time, knowing that her sister should have reached her house long before that time. She was so worried but could not go out because of the bad weather; and to make matters worse, Adeline's phone was not receiving calls; It was off.

Then a woman appeared from nowhere near the scene of the accident. She was frantically stopping any car that passed by, even though only two had driven pass on very high speed. The woman was restless, tossing back and forth and looking in all directions. Then she saw another car approaching. She quickly removed her scarf and started flagging the car. The driver drove past her, and then stopped about five meters away and reversed to where the woman was standing. It was a male driver and his wife was also sitting in front of the car. He slid down his window and asked if the woman needed help.

"Help my daughter please, help my daughter." The woman was in tears, but it was hard to know if it was tears or rain drops. She looked frenzied. There was blood on her forehead and her hand; and her skirt was torn on the left side. She could barely speak, but was audible enough to say her daughter needed assistance. She pointed to the car in the ditch and pleaded with the man to call for help. She just kept saying "my daughter, please, my daughter!"

The man made a few phone calls, probably calling the police and some friends to come to the scene. Then he decided to go down to the valley himself. He called out to his wife to remain in the car, but if she saw any approaching vehicle, she should signal it to stop and help. Steadily and carefully the man descended to the valley and saw the car inside. He went straight to the back seat and spotted the little girl trapped on her seat with the belt, seemingly in a deep sleep. She was unconscious.

He carefully removed the belt from the kid and took her out of the car. The car was twisted at the front and he was wondering what had happened to the driver. While holding the little girl with both hands, the Good Samaritan peeped into the car at the driver's seat. He saw a woman at the steering. He looked closely and saw that there was blood on her forehead, her right hand was equally covered with blood, and her dress was torn.

She was frantically stopping any car that passed by.

From all indications she had hit her head on the steering wheel and then fallen back on her seat; but she was motionless. He sent his hand and shook her but there was no reaction. She was … dead.

The man looked around whether he was dreaming or awake. "Is this not the same woman who had stopped me on the road and asked for help? Is it not the same bleeding face, same dress, same shape, same woman?" He shook himself and almost dropped the kid. Then he gathered enough courage and ran up the valley to the road, three-year -old unconscious kid in hand.

When he got to his wife she quickly took the kid from him, seeing that he was trembling. He asked where the injured woman was, but his wife could not explain. She said the woman was there a few minutes earlier, and then moved some distance away: did he not see her?

The man was perplexed. He did not know if he should express his thoughts. How could someone talk to you, and a few minutes later you find her body cold - in a trapped car? It then dawned on him that he had been dealing with the dead spirit of the woman. "Is this really true? Is it happening to him?" he thought.

A few minutes later the police arrived, and the woman's corpse was taken to the Mortuary. Her daughter however, survived the shock, and was discharged from the hospital a week later. Yes, that woman's spirit had saved her daughter.

A mother would go to all lengths to keep her children safe from danger; and will do everything in her power to make sure her children are alive. Even in their graves, mothers do not give up on the welfare of their kids. Some will even offer their lives in exchange for their young ones.

QUESTIONS

1. Give two reasons why Adeline decided to drive on even though the road was slippery?

2. Choose the phrase that has the same meaning as Good Samaritan:

    a.   A man from Samaria.

    b.   A Kind person

    c.   An Innocent woman

    d.   A fast driver

3. Give two lessons that you have learnt from the story.

4. Just like Adeline, many of you visit your sisters or friends. Write down three (3) topics of discussion during such visits.

5. Choose one character from the story and explain how he/she behaves like your family member.

6. go back and colour the picture on page 47.

It is often said that the snake was born with hands, but it was so lazy that it refused to use its hands to do anything useful, saying that when it grew older, it would work. When the time came for it to work, it could do nothing because its creator had taken the hand and given to those in need.

Jessica was a twelve-year-old girl and the second child among four, who lived with her aunt in the city. She was very naughty and stubborn, and refused to do any house chores. She often said there were older girls and boys in the house, and that when she grew older, she too would assist the younger ones; but until then, she had no other business at home than to eat, sleep and watch movies. Her aunt had complained several times to her mom, and tried to make Jessica become more involved to no avail. Years went by and Jessica became more mature. She was then seventeen and in High School, but still very lazy. Since each person is gifted with something better than others, Jessica was blessed with intellectual capacity. She was the most brilliant girl in her family, and everyone was always proud of her whenever examinations were concerned. She would score very high marks while the next person in class would be far behind her.

When Jessica finally enrolled into University, she had to live alone. She was very excited and anxious. Finally she could have liberty from her aunt and her house chores. She decided to live with her friend, Petra, who had promised to help her with cleaning and cooking.

Being a grown up already, Jessica knew that it was unacceptable for a girl her age to always eat out of home or to depend on others for her satisfaction. She was always hungry and became very lean because her allowance was too small for her to continuously buy food.

She decided one day to cook. Her choice fell on potatoes and beans. She bought some Irish potatoes and took home. She washed the potatoes and put in a pot, added water and let it boil. After a while, she washed the beans and put on the other side of the stove. A few minutes later she added salt, pepper, groundnut oil and other spices, and then she added water and let it to boil.

After an hour, Jessica was satisfied that the beans was ready. She turned off the stove, made a few calls and shortly after, three friends walked in, amongst them was her fiancé.

She happily served her guests the food and sat back to enjoy her own portion as she usually did when other people cooked for her. The first girl took a spoonful and declared that she did not think she would eat because she just had lunch. The second friend, James, also excused himself after a few mouthfuls, saying he was a patient and did not eat beans; but Jessica's fiancé, Bernard, could not hide the truth from her.

Jessica decided to cook potatoes and beans.

He pretended to be enjoying the meal and asked who did such "fantastic" cooking. Jessica happily said she did, and that she did it for him. Then he opened up. Bernard told Jessica how he was very disappointed in her; he could not believe that a beautiful girl like her was unable to cook a simple meal of potato and beans. Bernard told her that the beans was hard, the salt in the food was excessive, and the food itself was not appetizing. He told her to read her friends' facial expressions and know that they did not eat because the food was tasteless, not because they weren't hungry or sick as they had told her. He said all that and walked out of her room.

When Bernard left, Jessica could not stop crying. She wept for long and was filled with so much shame that she stayed home for two days, unable to face her friends.

You know, my friends, it is never too early or too late to learn. As a child, learn to assist people, so that when you grow up, you'll be useful to yourself and to others.

QUESTIONS

1. How many characters are in this story?

2. Who will you blame for Jessica's laziness?

A)   Her aunt   C) Her father

B)   Her mother   D) Herself

3. Choose another word below that sounds the same
   as "proud".

A)   Vowel

B)   Pride

C)   Crowd

D)   Boast

4. What lesson(s) have you learnt from this story?

5. Do you know anyone who is in the same situation
   as Jessica? What advice will you give him/her?

8 MY GUARDIAN ANGEL

Prayer is the key that opens all doors; and the Holy Book entreats us to pray at all times. Everything dedicated to God through prayer is protected by the spirit of light from the invisible world. And that is why when you dedicate yourself to the Lord each day, He puts angels to watch and guard over you through hills and valleys.

The story is told of a little ten-year-old girl, Marie-Therese, who was returning from school on a certain Wednesday all by herself. Her brothers had stayed back at school because they had to take extra classes in Mathematics.

Marie-Therese was quite anxious to get home because her mother, a nurse, was not working on that particular day and she knew a very delicious meal was awaiting her. And so she decided to use a short cut to her house which was about fifteen minutes walk from school.

As the little girl approached the bridge that curved from the school vicinity, she spotted a tall man of about twenty-six years sitting on the rails of the bridge. He was concentrating on a bird eating grains of corn nearby. The man was dressed in a worn-out blue shirt and black trousers. Without reducing her steps and without moving her lips, Marie-Therese made a silent prayer:

"Lord God my Shepherd,
You are always there for me,
Lead me home safely,
In Jesus name,
Amen."

As she sang the new song that her teacher had taught her, she noticed that the man was looking at her. She simply greeted him and went her way, and got home safe and sound.

Later that evening, while her parents were watching The Evening News, they heard something awful that had happened in their neighbourhood. Marie's father called them to join him and watch the news. A girl of about ten had been murdered at that

Someone wearing a white sparkling robe was
walking by her and he could not go close to her.

same bridge that led to her house that afternoon. The police had arrested a man who was about twenty-six years old. Marie-Therese immediately recognized the man as the same person she had seen and greeted on her way back from school that afternoon.

When interviewed why he had committed such a gruesome act, the murderer said he had planned to kill any child between ten and thirteen years old on that day. He said another little girl had passed by earlier on, and he had targeted that girl; but that when she approached the bridge, someone wearing a white sparkling robe was walking by her and he could not go close to her; so he fell on the next victim who came his way.

Marie-Therese was amazed. "Hmm dad, I used that short-cut today, so could this man be talking about me? Does he mean that an Angel was walking by me when he saw me? Was that my Guardian Angel?" she asked a series of questions. "Yes, Marie", her mom replied. "Your Guardian Angel was taking care of you."

I tell you, each time you call upon the Lord in prayer, He will answer you. You may find yourself walking alone in a dark street, but know that when you pray, the Angel of the Lord will either carry you through the valley of the shadow of death, or walk by you to keep you from hurting your feet. Therefore pray without ceasing, for this is the will of God.

QUESTIONS

1. Why was the girl returning from school all by herself?
2. Describe the man that the girl saw as she approached the bridge.
3. How did Marie-Therese learn about the murder of the girl?
4. How would you have reacted if you were Marie-Therese?
5. Give one theme that runs through this story.

9   THE LONESOME MAN

A fly that does not listen to advice follows the corpse into the grave. It is always very easy for someone to see that other people are living fulfilled lives, while he/she is suffering. We look around and see the fabulous cars that others drive, the mansions that they build or live in, the elaborate parties they throw and wish we were in their shoes. We never bother to ask questions or to even know about them.

Pa Moses has been an old man in the eyes of the youths for a very long time. He lived in a small thatch house in the village all by himself. As children, we always wondered where his wife and children were. Why was he alone? It was very absurd to find a man living by himself in a community where every-one seemed to be related to the other.

One day, my father told me about the life of Pa Moses. He said Pa Moses was once married and lived in Mokonje village with his wife and two kids, both boys. He was a very neat man because he had once served as a steward to a white man, and so had to always look clean .

Pa Moses had married his wife, Relindis, from his native village and taken her to Mokonje; and she was a very lovable young woman.

After only three years of marriage, Relindis felt that her husband was too old for her. She had become exposed to city life and wanted to live a fabulous lifestyle like other young girls. She started buying very expensive dresses, went out late and made friends with unmarried girls who had no kids and husbands to look after. She wore make-up and high heeled shoes that looked very dazzling. Relindis had suddenly become so beautiful that even neigh-bours wondered where she got all the money from to buy such expensive items. If she wanted something and her husband said he did not have the money, she would appear the next day with it and would give no explanation as to how she got it.

Pa Moses was a very neat man.

Before long, Relindis' demands were too many for her husband to cope with. He told her that she was very extravagant and had to cut her coat according to her cloth. This infuriated Relindis to the point that she decided to pack out of her husband's house. She told him that she was tired of living in misery with an old fool like him, and that she would find another man who would marry her and provide her needs. Her husband begged her to stay and take care of their two kids but she did not heed to his plea. She told him that her mind was made-up.

Months went by and Pa Moses did not see his wife anymore. He later heard that she was living in a big house in the city. She had sneaked into the compound one day in his absence and taken the two boys away. They were now already five and seven years old. When he returned and did not see the boys, Moses raised an alarm; but his boss, Petes, told him that the kids' mother had come for them. From that day, Moses started looking for his children. After a year, he decided to go to the city again for the fourth time. This time he spent two weeks looking for Relindis. He looked in all the nooks and crannies of the city, but luck was not on his side. He asked everyone who bothered to listen to him if they had seen any girl moving about with two little boys. Many people just laughed and told him that the city was too busy for one to take note of such trivial matters.

Then one day he bombed into his first son. The boy was trying to cross the road when he saw his father and recognized him. Imagine how excited the lad was to see his father after such a long while.

"Papa! Papa!" He shouted. Moses turned to see his son running towards him. He ran towards his son and embraced the kid with so much passion and love, tears running down his cheeks - tears of joy.
"Where is your brother?" he asked.
"At home," the innocent kid answered, "with Mum and Uncle Petes."
"Uncle Petes? Who is Uncle Petes?" Moses wondered aloud.

Moses followed his son to 'their house', and to his greatest dismay, met his boss, Petes, relaxing in the living room. It suddenly dawned on him that his wife had left him for his boss. Petes was the one who had lured his innocent wife out of her marital home with gifts and goodies; rented her a place in the city, arranged for her to collect her kids in his absence, and was then living with her. He could not believe it! He felt so disgusted. He grabbed his kids and made for the door, then changed his mind and brought them back, and then left the house in total rage.

When he returned to Mokonje, Moses immediately gathered his belongings and returned to his village. He lived there ever after, refusing to remarry for fear of having another heart break.

Five years later, however, Relindis returned to the village very sick. She had been abandoned in the city after two years by Mr. Petes who had fled with her children. She did not know where to find neither him nor her boys. She had remained in the city for three full years, waiting and hoping that they will return. They never did. Her friends then advised her to find ways of surviving in the city because they were tired of looking after her. In the process of trying to fend for herself, she contracted Chlamydia and HIV/AIDS.

Back in the village she became a laughing stock, despised by her family members and shunned by friends. The village square, homes and farms echoed with work songs composed about Relindis and her waywardness; and she could not stand the embarrassment. Three months later she died, more from misery and shame, than from the illness that she was suffering from.

Be content with what you have, my friends, for all that glitters is not gold.

QUESTIONS

1. Name all the characters in this story.

2. The story has several places where it is set. Name three.

3. Give the meaning of the following words as used in the story:

    a) Fabulous

    b) Absurd

    c) Exposed

    d) Dazzling

4. Explain the following phrases:

    a) Cut her coat according to her cloth.

    b) All that glitters is not gold.

5. Explain briefly the reasons for Relindis' return to the village.

6. Many youths do wrong things because of their exposure to city life. List three (3) of such unethical behaviours.

10 FANNY AND THE RICH MAN

Many years ago in a small village called Nfuni in Cameroon, lived a quiet farmer popularly known as Manboy. Manboy had the misfortune of owing a large sum of money to a shrewd village money-lender. The money-lender, Chopdie, who was old and ugly, fancied the farmer's beautiful daughter, Fanny, and had been eyeing her ever since she became of age. So he proposed a bargain. He said he would forgo Manboy's debt only if he could marry Manboy's daughter.

Both Manboy and Fanny were horrified by that proposal and thus refused the suggestion. So the cunning money-lender, Pa Chopdie, suggested that they let providence decide the matter. They will play a game in which the winner comes out victorious all round.

Pa Chopdie told them that he would put one black and one white pebble into an empty bag. Then the girl would have to pick a pebble from the bag. If she picked the black pebble, she would become his wife and her father's debt would be cancelled. If she picked the white pebble instead, she need not marry him and her father's debt would still be annulled. However, if she refused to pick a pebble, her father would be thrown into jail.

Being a very loving daughter who did not want her father to end up in prison, and knowing that her father did not have the money to pay back, Fanny decided to go along with the old man's proposal. Manboy was furious, calling the old shrewd names and pulling his daughter away. But Fanny calmed her father, saying *he who pays the piper calls the tune.* She told her father that she would do any-thing to save him from further disgrace; and that every test in one's life happens so as to make the person bitter or better, but the choice is ours, whether we want to let ourselves become victims or victors.

Fanny fumbled with the pebble and let it fall.

The trio was standing in an open field at the village school compound, near a new classroom under construction. Their loud voices and arguments had attracted passers-by and a little crowd had gathered some distance away and stood as witnesses to Chopdie's drama, amongst them was Silas.

Silas was the village drunk who knew all the happenings around the community. He could tell you what each person in the village was planning to do or what they had done even in hiding. Those who knew Silas did not et him interfere in their affairs because he always told the truth without fear or favour. "Be vigilant with that crook", Silas cautioned Fanny in an offhanded manner, "he is always cheating on people so as to have his way". Fanny heard and took note of the drunk's words, and that made her more vigilant.

As they talked, Pa Chopdie opened the bag and showed the girl and her father, assuring them that nothing else was in the bag. He then bent over to pick up the two pebbles. As he picked them up, the sharp-eyed girl noticed that he had instead picked two black pebbles and put them into the bag. He then asked the girl to make her choice from the bag. No other person had been observant enough, not even Manboy who was standing next to the old man.

The girl put her hand into the money bag and drew out a pebble. Everyone present was just holding their hearts in their palms. Manboy's heart was beating so fast that you could literally see his chest pounding. Without looking at it, Fanny fumbled with the pebble that she had just picked from the bag and let it fall onto the pebble-strewn path where it immediately became lost among all the other pebbles. "Oh my gosh, how clumsy of me!" she exclaimed. "You are really clumsy!!!" snapped the money lender, "to be so careless as not to be able to handle a tiny little object. I wonder how you plan to till the soil and pound cocoyam for my meals." "Who will pound you cocoyam?," Manboy asked in fury. "Do you think I'll let you go away with this? No way!!!!. The Chief must hear this and justice will take its course."

There was a heated exchange of harsh words between the two men, with the on-lookers shouting and cursing the money-lender, who did not care about their annoyance; all he wanted was a young wife for an exchange of his money.

"He is nothing but a cheat," Silas shouted from the crown. "And you Manboy, don't you know that a Grassbird does not play hide-and-seek with a Bat at night? I am telling you, Chopdie will ..." The crowd hushed Silas down.

Then Fanny chipped in: "But never mind, if you look into the bag for the pebble that is left, you will be able to tell which pebble I picked. Manboy got up from the ground where he was crawled awaiting his daughter's fate. "Open the bag let us see the other pebble", he said with a nervous voice. He had been praying silently for God to vindicate him, but more for his daughter to be liberated.

Pa Chopdie knew his trick had failed, but he dared not admit his dishonesty. He opened the bag, and to the extreme delight of everyone present, what came out was a black pebble, meaning that Fanny was not going to marry the old man, and Manboy was still freed from his debts. The girl had just changed what seemed an impossible situation into an extremely advantageous one.

LESSON

Do not fret over the difficulties that come your way, just think of how to handle each problem because every difficulty has a solution.

QUESTIONS

1. Where is this story set?

2. How many characters are there in this story?

3. Why did the girl let the pebble that she picked from the bag drop?

4. a) Now, imagine that you were standing in the field. What would you have done if you were Fanny?

   b) If you had to advise her, what would you have told her?

5. Write down three (3) sentences about what you think happened immediately afterward.

11 SPECIAL SUMMONS

It is said that the head of a foolish man is found in his mouth, but the mouth of a wise man is found in his head. There lived a man who was never happy with what he got. He was a widower. He had got married quite early in his youth, but was not blessed with any off-springs. He however raised many family children, some had grown big and got married, others were still in the village with him, though living in their own houses, and others were nowhere to be seen.

Papa Emman, as he was called, really never lacked anything. Even though he lived alone, his 'children' took turns in caring for him. Each day they made sure one of them took food to him; or sent their children to fetch water and sweep his house. He always appreciated the children with little gifts like banana and/or oranges, and would advise them to be good and obedient children, yet he was always unhappy.

Everybody in the village knew that Papa Emman had not been happy ever since he lost his wife. He kept to himself more and more; neither ate nor drank village food, and went to his farm at very odd hours. It was customary for villagers to go to the farm very early in the morning, so that by mid day when the sun was overhead, they were already returning home; the women with bundles of wood on their heads, others with a basin of cassava or coco-yams, and the men just lazing along with machetes in hand. However Papa Emman was no longer part of this custom. He went to the farm at mid day, and only returned at night fall, bringing along nothing to show that he was coming from his farm.

One of his sons, Effoe, became suspicious of his moves. He asked himself several questions: why did his father go to the farm only when others were returning? Why didn't he come back home with any food? Did he actually work in his farm? And why did he keep so much to himself? Effoe decided to trail Pa Emman since his farm was next to his father's.

He started leaving for the farm just about the same time as his father.

The first day Effoe was surprised to see what his father wasted his time in the farm doing. Papa Emman got to the farm shortly after him, and after clearing a small portion of land, he went and sat under a large tree. The tree had far-spreading branches and so served as a shade. The leaves on the branches were green and full, and one could hardly see through. He sat there for sometime just hitting his cutlass on one spot. And then started talking to no one in particular.

He bemoaned his situation and asked the angel of death to have pity on him and take him away from this world. He wondered why his gods kept him alive to be suffering when all his age mates had died and gone to meet their wives. He was very depressed, and called on death to visit him right there. After saying all these, he stretched himself on the ground under the tree and fell asleep. An hour or so later, he got up, dusted himself, and asked the invisible companion if he was still alive; he shook his legs to be sure, and then stood up, picked up his machete and left for the village. Effoe followed him at a distance until they got to the village and they both went to their respective homes.

The next day Effoe followed his father to the farm again and observed the same scenario. This went on for five days, each day Effoe thought Pa Emman would do something different, but nothing changed. So he thought to himself that he must take some action to stop what his father was doing; but what could he do without reproaching the old man. After searching his mind, he came up with a plan.

The next day he got to the farm an hour before his father. He had brought with him a medium size white bed sheet, white gloves and white socks. He climbed up the tree that usually served as Papa Emman's shade and positioned himself just above where his father usually sat. Then he carefully wrapped the sheet around his shoulders, wore the white gloves and socks, and sat quietly waiting.

'Look at me, I have worked all my life in vain',
Papa Emman complained.

Pa Emman arrived a little late on that fateful day. In fact, Effoe was almost climbing down, thinking that he had made a fruitless plan when his target arrived. Unlike other days, he went straight to the tree and sat under it and started recounting his frustration: "Look at me, I have worked all my life in vain; no wife, no children, no decent house, no companion. I am fed up with such life. I cannot continue like this. Death where are you? Come and take me, I want to go. God please send your angel to come and rescue me, my time is up. I want to …"

Before he could continue with his lamentations, Effoe just intervened using a very angelic voice. He spread out his hands and feet, with the white bed sheet spreading behind him like an angel. He was hanging on one branch of the tree, legs spread to another branch, face covered:

"I have come, my son; I have come to your rescue. You have called upon my name for too long, and I have come to answer your prayer. Your suffering is over this day, my son! Come with me now, come let

me take you home!!! No more farms, no more hunger. I am here, come!!! Come!!!"

Pa. Emman carried up his head and saw an angel spread over him on the tree, hands out-stretched, beckoning on him. He could not believe that "the angel of death" had actually come to take him away. He was perplexed.

He gathered all the strength that he had left and got up from the ground. Before he had time to think, he was already out of his farm. He ran for about a mile before realizing that he had forgotten to take his machete, but the thought of going back to get it did not as much as cross his mind.

He stopped to regain his breath when he saw some women resting on the road side. They were all surprised to see an old man running from nothing. When asked, he simply said: "tell him I have changed my mind; I love my life as it is," and then he started running again. The women were confused, but no one followed to get an explanation.

For the next two days following the incident, Papa Emman did not go to the farm. Effoe visited him each of those days, bringing along food and palm wine. To his greatest surprise, his father ate the food without complaining and was unusually nice to everyone who stopped by. It was only on the third day that Pa. Emman gathered a few family members and told them what had happened to him; concluding that he would never step his feet on that particular farm any more. All who listened to him sighed with relief.

You see dear friends, life has its ups and downs, but each of us should learn to accept our fate. Stop complaining about your life because your situation may be better than that of most people around you. Just live a positive life and it will be well with you.

QUESTIONS

1. How many characters do we find in this story?

2. Give three other words from the story which sound the same as "nothing".

3. Pick out five nouns and five adjectives from the story.

4. What role did Effoe play in restoring his father's joy?

5. Make sentences with the following words:
     a. Appreciate
     b. Plant
     c. Companion
     d. Spread
     e. Beckon.

6. If your father behaves like Mr. Emman, what action will you take?

12   WATCH YOUR TONGUE

Hilary was a fourteen-year-old boy with a very bad temper. He got angry about everything and anything. Worse still, whenever he was angry, he would do something that usually left a mark of his anger. For instance, once he went to school and his classmate took his pen from the teacher's table and was using without asking permission from Hilary. When the French teacher came to class, Hilary could not copy his notes because he did not have a pen. So the teacher asked him to stand behind the class as punishment until the end of the lesson. When Hilary later found his pen with Simeon, he flared with anger. He seized the pen, pointed it at Simeon, and before Simeon could explain that he (Hilary) forgot taking it from the Maths teacher who had borrowed it to correct her notes, Hilary broke the pen and pierced his friend on the arm twice. This, of course, ended him serious punishment and a letter of apology to Simeon.

Hilary's parents, Mr. and Mrs. Chemi had struggled to control their son's anger with very little success. They had beaten him several times, locked him up in the room for hours, but he did not change! They refused to give him food for being rude and irritable, still there was no success. They even went to his school to punish him in front of all his class-mates; that made matters worse!!!

One day Mr. Chemi had an idea on how to deal with his son's anger. Hilary was playing football outside with his elder brother when the brother screamed for help. When their mom went to the scene, Hilary claimed that his brother was cheating and scoring unacceptable goals. So in anger he took the ball and stamped it on his brother's face.

Mr. Chemi was outraged with this conduct. He took a bag of 15 inches nails. There were more than 200 nails in the bag. He handed the bag and a hammer to his son, Hilary, and showed him a wall that formed part of the fence of their house.

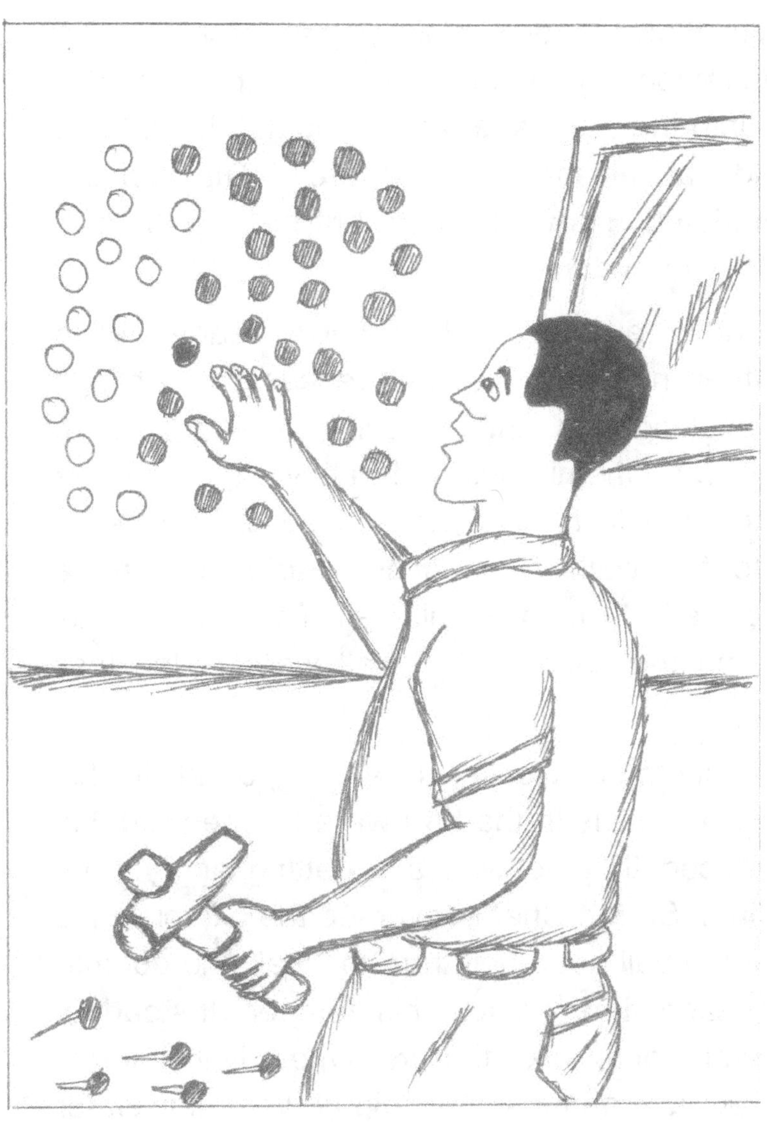

Hilary pulled out a nail from the wall
each time he lost his temper.

He then instructed Hilary that each time he loses his temper, he should use the hammer and drill one nail into the wall as far as he could. If he did not, he would be punished very severely. That punishment infuriated Hilary so much, but he had to carry out his father's orders.

Within an hour Hilary had already drilled about fifteen nails into the wall because his siblings were provoking him, thus causing him to flare-up with rage. Mr. Chemi could not believe it, but by the end of that week, his son had drilled close to sixty nails into the wall. Then Hilary started making a conscious effort to hold himself from losing his temper and the nails on the wall were drilled less frequently.

After three weeks, Hilary reported to his father that the nails in the bag were finished, but his father noticed that he was still getting angry from time to time. So Mr. Chemi reversed the exercise. He told Hilary to pull out a nail from the wall and put into the bag each time he lost his temper. Instead of getting really angry like the first time, Hilary merely wore a sad face and said it would be very difficult for him to pull out the nails because he had buried them deep into the wall. Another tool was handed to him to ease his job.

So Hilary pulled out a nail from time to time. Gradually he realized that a day or two went by without him pulling out a nail from the wall. At the end it took him three months to pull out the 200 nails that he had drilled into the wall in just three weeks. At last the nails were all out and he reported this to his father with a smile.

But Mr. Chemi was not done with his son yet. He took Hilary to the wall and showed him the holes that he had burst on the wall; and how much damage he had caused. The next task therefore was for him to fill the holes and make sure no mark remained to show that there was ever a hole on that spot. Each time he lost his temper again, he would fill one hole. Mr. Chemi was expecting Hilary to flare up in anger and frustration, but Hilary simply turned and told his father that it was impossible to fill the holes without leaving a mark, and he said this in a calm and respectful manner. Mr. Chemi was particularly pleased because his son could control his anger and had also become well-mannered. He took his son by the hand and said to him:

"You see my son, each time you use harsh words on people, or inflict pain on someone, know that you have drilled a nail into someone who loves you. When you say you are sorry, you have removed the nail, but the scars remain in the person's mind, and even if you work hard towards covering the scars, your efforts will always be fruitless. So it is best not to use harsh words."

Dear friends, anger can push us to do terrible things, and we will always regret afterwards. We must therefore control our temper in every situation no matter how much we are provoked. This is because when you lose your temper and say something dreadful or horrifying, there is no way to take back your words. You may say you are sorry, but that does not mean that the pain or scar which you inflicted on the person has been wiped out. No!!!

Subsequently, when next you get angry and throw harsh words on your friends and loved ones, remember that people who live in glass houses should not throw stones.

QUESTIONS

1. Suggest another title for this story.

2. Was Hilary justified to pierce his classmate Simeon?

3. Use one word to describe each of these characters; the first one has been done for you:

No.	Character	Description
a	Hilary	Aggressive
b	Simeon	
c	Mr. Chemi	
d	Hilary	

4. What did Mr. Chemi ask Hilary to do and why?

5. What lesson did Hilary learn after the punishment?

6. Give two lessons that you have learnt from this story.

13   THE BLISSFUL UNION

After twenty years of marriage to her husband, Etengene recounted this story to her children one day. She was very fond of telling stories and actually found pleasure when the family was gathered in the evening listening to each other. Today, she decided to tell how she met their dad.

"It was my mother's funeral," she started. "My mother had been a very generous and compassionate woman. She was always there when I needed her. I knew that she prayed for me during my entire life. My mother had been blessed with three lovely children, two daughters and a son. I, Etengene, was the second of the trio. This name was given to me because I was born "legs first". In my custom, special names are given to particular births. If a woman has twins for example, the children are named Ayamba, meaning "first-in-line", and Manyo meaning "next-in-line". Everyone knows that twins come with their names and they are named as soon as they are delivered. Any child delivered after the twins is called Nkongho, which means "follower of twins". But I was named Etengene which is a name given to a child who comes into the world with the legs first, instead of the head.

My elder sister had just had a baby when our mother got seriously ill, and my younger brother was recently married. I had no entanglements, thus it was I who could fully devote my time to take care of our mother during the many months of illness; and this, I consider, was an honour.

After one year and seven months, my mother passed away and I found myself completely lost. What was I to do with my life then? I thought and felt emptiness inside me.

At the funeral I was heartbroken with no one to console me. Then I looked at my brother, he sat frigidly, clutching his wife's hand. She would console him from time to time and made sure he did not feel too depressed. My sister sat by her husband and cuddled their baby. He held his arms around her, and the baby smiled at her all the time; forcing her to smile back once or twice.

I sat alone, grieving so deeply. Nobody noticed that I was in anguish and had no one to talk to, even my mother's relatives did not seem to care about my feelings. My mother had been my closest friend. We played cards and told stories together; I prepared our meals, helped with her visits to the doctors and took her to village meetings once in a while when her health permitted. Now my job was done and I was all alone again. I looked up to the cross at the altar and prayed, "Lord be my companion".

Suddenly I heard quick footsteps hurrying along the floor. In a moment I saw a young man, his eyes were filled with tears which he could not hold back. He sat next to me. Then he sniffled: "I'm late" and then added: "Why do they call her by a different name?" I whispered, "Because that was her name". I wondered why this stranger sat next to me and interrupted my grieving with his tears and fidgeting.

"Her name is Mami Sarah, but the pastor keeps

saying Ma Alice," he said.

"Yes, her name is Alice," I replied.

Then a sudden thought struck his mind.

"Emm, Is this Ebenezer Baptist church?"

"Nooo, Ebenezer is across the street. This is Native Baptist Church".

It was clear that the man was at the wrong funeral. This awkward situation and solemnity of the funeral bubbled up inside me, I began to laugh. I tried to stop myself but couldn't. Some mourners threw sharp looks at me. I turned and looked at the man sitting next to me, he started laughing too. "Well, I guess I'll just stay here and finish this service", he said amidst his laughter.

I imagined my mother watching us and laughing together with us, because she too was fond of laughing at people's shortcomings.

I began to laugh. I tried to stop myself but could not.

After the final "Amen", we went out together to the church courtyard where the hearse that was to convey the corpse was stationed. "Perhaps we will be the talk of the town," he said to me, smiling, and then offered, "Since I have missed my aunt's funeral, maybe we could have a drink some time after the burial?" I agreed.

A year after the embarrassing church laughter, we got married at the same small Native Baptist church. This time we both arrived at the right place. God gave me laughter and love in my time of sorrow. Now we are celebrating our twentieth wedding anniversary. Each time somebody asks us how we met, your daddy always tells them: "Her mother and my aunt introduced us to each other". Thus, our match was certainly made in heaven."

The saying goes that when God closes one door, he opens another, sometimes wider than the first. The happiness that you think you lack now will be doubled when the right time comes, Just commit everything to God in prayer.

QUESTIONS

1. How many siblings did Etengene have?

2. Why was she lonely at the funeral?

3. Give the name of the stranger who came and sat next to Etengene.

4. Give the meaning of the following words as used in the story:
    a) Companion
    b) Sniffled
    c) Fidgeting
    d) Awkward

5. Comment on the special names in your society that have particular meanings.

14   THE TWO FRIENDS

Peter and his classmate, Brandon, were always picking on each other for practically everything that they came across or knew about. They argued about their school bags, their parents' educational level, which of their teachers was more competent, and even about the food that their mothers prepared back at home. Many people were surprised that they were able to make amends after each disagreement and went on with their friendship as if nothing had gone wrong.

On this particular day, the squabble was about who invented the first wheelchair. Brandon said it was Harry Jennings, but Peter was so sure it was Herbert Everest. He knew that he had read somewhere that it was the Chinese who should be given the credit because they had used wheelbarrows and moved disabled persons around, thereby giving engineers the initiative of coming up with a wheelchair. He could not remember the exact name of the Chinese but intended to find out and tell Brandon the next day. Many of their classmates did not know who the inventor actually is, so they became indifferent and left, but the two friends would not let go their points.

Peter was convinced that he was right and Brandon was wrong – and Brandon was just as convinced that Peter was wrong and he was right. They decided to take the matter to their Physics master for a solution. Unfortunately the master was out for other duties and the History master could not help them out. Then the Dean of studies decided to put a stop to their constant wrangling by using her own judicious approach.

She took the whole class to the Science Laboratory and brought up Peter and Brandon to the front of the lab. At the far end of the room was a machine which had been out of use for close to two years. The Dean asked the two boys to push the machine to the front, and to make no stop until they got to the position designed for that object. This they did, glancing from time to time at their giggling class-mates.

Now placed where everyone could see, the Dean asked the two boys to stand on either side of the machine and say what shape it was. Brandon told the class with such simplicity that it was square. Peter looked at him with disbelief; and when asked, Peter said it was round. Brandon gasped with skepticism and said in a louder tone SQUARE!!! Peter shouted round!!! square!!! round!!!

Before they could start another round of square/round squabble, the Dean stopped them and asked that they move positions. Then she asked the same question to both of them, this time starting with Peter. "What shape is the machine?" Peter opened his mouth to say 'round' and then caught himself mid-way when he realized that he was actually seeing the machine as being square. He looked at the shape more closely, and then very slowly and reluctantly said 'sq-u-a-r-eee'.

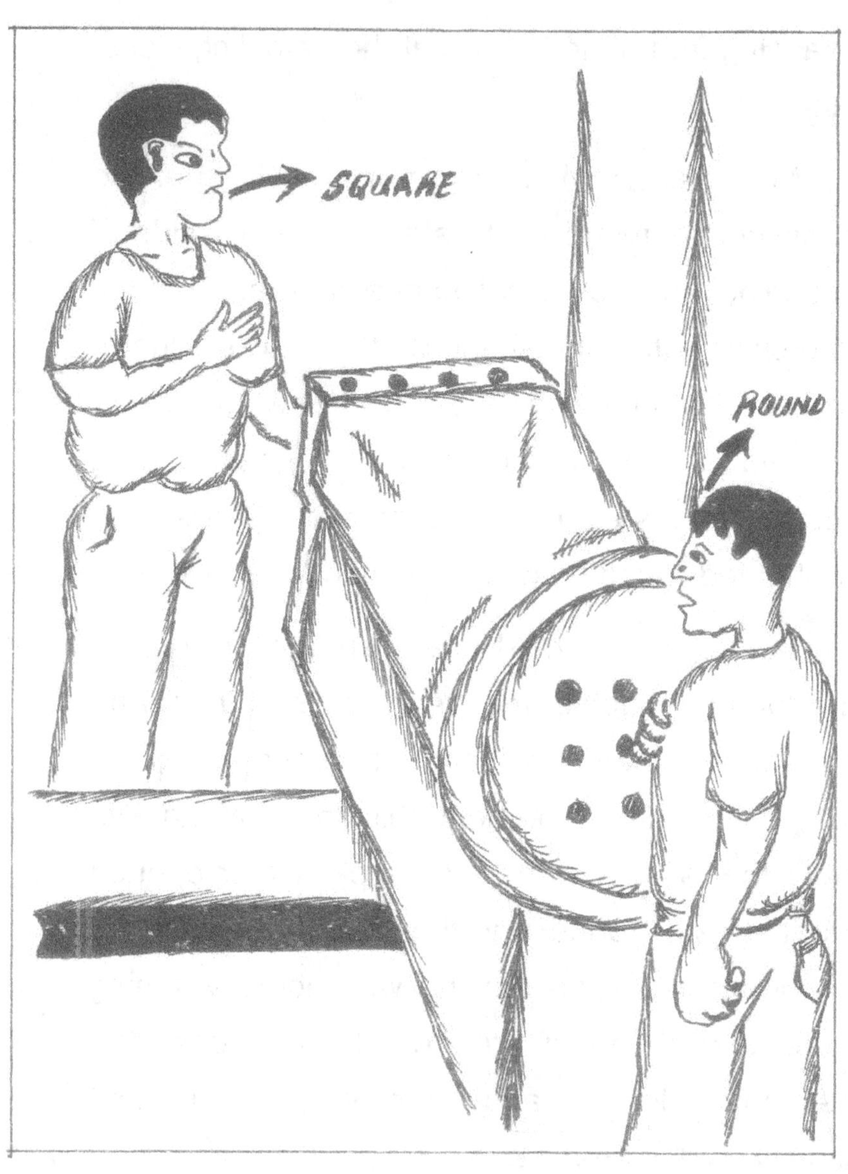

Peter said ROUND; Brandon shouted SQUARE!

Brandon did not offer any word, but everyone present could see the disbelief in his expression. He could not belief that an object that he had seen as square, with his own eyes, had suddenly become round. Without asking for permission, he moved back to his former position and looked; it was square, then he crossed to the other side, and it was round. Then he asked aloud, "how can this be?"

The Dean explained, "You see, this machine has been placed there because it has caused a lot of confusion in our students' minds, and caused many to fail their exams. Things do not always turn out the way they are meant to be, or the way human eyes must perceive them. This machine has been kept there to illustrate to us that there can be many confusing things in life; and our viewpoints are not always right. So when next you get into a brawl, consider the other persons standpoint because he is not an empty vessel. Listen to others, because "even the dull and the ignorant, they too have their story".

QUESTIONS

1. Name three things that the two friends quarreled about.

2. Where is the story set?

3. Give other words from the passage that have the same number of syllables as the following:

No.	Word	No. of syllables	Another word with equal no. of syllables
a	Classmate	2	(example) Matter
b	Actually		
c	Laboratory		
d	Giggling		
e	Shape		
f	Indifferent		

4. Suggest another title for this story.

5. What conclusion would you draw from this story?

6. There are some of your classmates or friends who behave like Brandon, how do you cope with them?

15   THE VISITOR

There are some guests that announce their coming while others just pop into your house unannounced. Death is one such visitor who never announces his arrival, and whenever he gets into a house, the occupants would wail, run or even scream to the top of their voices. No one ever welcomes death for he is always an intruder who brings nothing but pain.

It came to pass that twenty-six year old Johnson was relaxing in his living room one day when he heard a knock at the door. He placed the book which he was reading on the couch and went to open the door. Standing before him was an elegant looking young man who requested to be allowed in. Johnson moved to the side and let the young man in without actually knowing who he was. But since he had been brought up to show respect and reverence for everybody he meets, Johnson decided not to ask any questions for fear of being rude.

The visitor picked up a very interesting conversation with his host. They discussed the novel that Johnson was reading, talked about the recent happenings in town and also about their personal lives. By that time the visitor had introduced himself as a friend to Johnson's elder brother.

While they were talking, Johnson entertained his guest with some food and drink, and again some snacks; and so after a while the visitor felt really tired and fell asleep on the couch. As he was removing the used items, Johnson noticed that his guest was holding a piece of paper on his hands with a list of names written on it. The people were shortlisted to die as their names appeared on the list; and Johnson's name was now the first name on the list because the first three names had been crossed out and written beside them, "mission accomplished".

It then dawned on Johnson that his visitor was death. He thought to himself about dying!!! "How could he die so young?" He asked himself.

What had he accomplished in life? Had he been in good terms with God? What will happen to his soul? All these questions went through Johnson's mind in a split of a second. "I have to do something about this! I can not just let death take me away; I must act, and fast!!!"

Johnson took the paper from death's hand while death was still asleep. He ran to the room and got an ink blotter. As quickly as he could, Johnson blotted out his name from the position where it was and swopped it with the name on the last position in the list. He was very cautious to get the exact hand-writing on the paper. Then he tiptoed back to the Living Room and placed the paper in death's hand just as it was. Death was still fast asleep.

Satisfied with his action, Johnson relaxed on his own couch and went back to his book. After a short while, death stretched out himself and got up from sleep, surprised that he had actually slept so deeply in a complete stranger's house. He smiled at his host and said to Johnson:

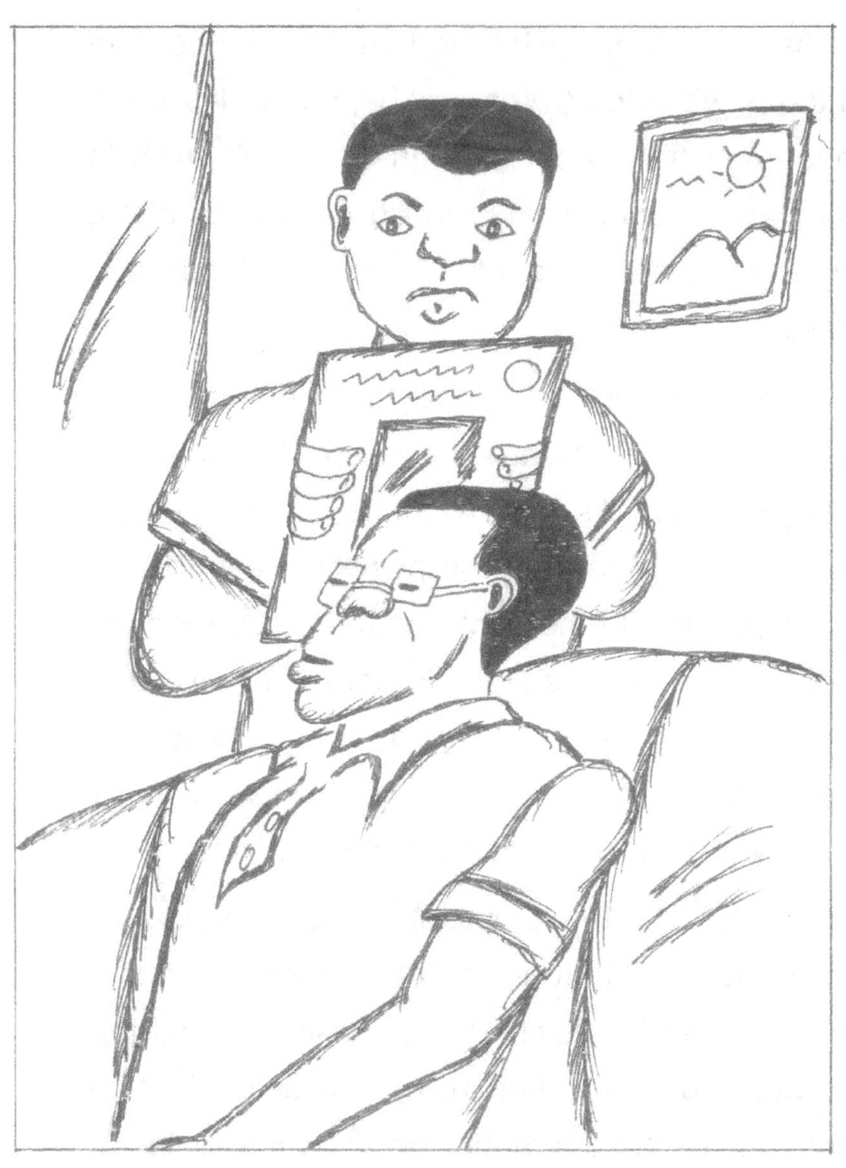

Johnson took the paper from Death's hand

"I have been visiting many dwellings and quarters, hospitals and healing homes, churches and beer parlours, but wherever I go people never welcome me. Sometimes I am stoned, other times I am cursed; and some other people just resign themselves and let me have my way. Nobody has ever welcomed me the way you have done today. I am truly impressed with your attitude.

"You see we had decided that today is your turn to leave this world and join your ancestors. I am not supposed to tell you this, but I do now because you are special. Since you received me with so much love and generosity, I have decided that I will instead take my victims from below because after your name it is your friend's, and then your mother's. So I will spare you all the trouble of mourning your loved ones. He turned the paper upside down and ticked the last name – and then wrote by it, "Mission accomplished". Johnson collapsed on the couch even before death had finished pronouncing his last sentence.

Dear friends, you can never buy your way through life by cheating. We are all called upon to live exemplary lives here on earth, keeping to the laws and instructions laid down, so that whenever we are called out of this world, we will know that we are ready for the world beyond.

QUESTIONS

1. Who is the visitor in this story?
2. Say three (3) issues that they discussed.
3. Why did the visitor fall asleep on the coach?
   a)   He was tired.
   b)   He needed rest.
   c)   He had over-fed himself.
   d)   He was angry with Johnson.
4. At the end, the story talks about cheating. How does Johnson try to cheat?
5. Say what you like or dislike about this story.

GLOSSARY

Mami Koki: A woman who sells koki to earn a living.

Bushfaller: One who travels abroad often.